Paddington
Minds the House

First published in hardback in Great Britain by HarperCollins Publishers Ltd in 1986
First published in paperback by Collins Lions in 2001
This edition published as part of a gift set by HarperCollins Children's Books in 2015

Collins Lions is an imprint of HarperCollins Publishers Ltd.
HarperCollins Children's Books is a division of HarperCollins Publishers Ltd.

Text copyright © Michael Bond 1986
Illustrations copyright © R. W. Alley 1999

Visit our website at: www.harpercollins.co.uk

Printed in China

Michael Bond

Paddington
Minds the House

Illustrated by R. W. Alley

HarperCollins *Children's Books*

One morning, Mrs Brown and Mrs Bird went out for the day and left Paddington to look after the house.

"I shall wash up all the breakfast things while you are gone," he said. "And then, if I have any time left over I may do some 'Spring Cleaning'."

"Oh dear," said Mrs Brown. "I don't like the sound of that!"

As soon as the others had gone, Paddington set to work. He washed all the breakfast cups and saucers and plates, and put them in a rack to dry.

Then he did the dusting, and after that he washed the dusters and the towels, and hung them up to dry.

When he had finished hanging up the dusters and towels, he started making a special chocolate cake as a surprise for Mrs Brown and Mrs Bird when they got back.

Paddington liked cooking, and he was soon busy mixing flour and cocoa and sugar and milk together in a large bowl.

It wasn't until he put his paw in the mixture to make sure it tasted as it should that he saw he had made a mess with the flour and cocoa. Worse still, the floor felt crunchy under his feet where he had spilt some sugar, so he got the vacuum cleaner out.

That was when his troubles started.

In his haste to tidy the kitchen he put the hose on the wrong end of the cleaner by mistake, and instead of sucking, it blew.

Paddington staggered back as all the old dust came out and rose into the air like a big, black cloud.

It landed everywhere: on the clean cups and saucers and plates, over the dusters and towels he had hung up to dry, over the table and chairs and floor. It even landed on his cake mix.

Paddington decided it was a good thing he was making a chocolate cake. At least it wouldn't show the dirt.

Paddington started work all over again.

He washed the breakfast things. Then he washed the dusters and the towels, and hung them up to dry.

And because the dusters were now wet, he thought he would use the vacuum cleaner to get rid of the dust.

This time he made sure the tube was on the right end.

Using the vacuum cleaner was much more fun and Paddington spent some time trying to write his name in the dust on top of the table.

It wasn't until he got as far as the letter 'd' that he noticed the mixing bowl was now empty.

He stared at the end of the hose wondering what to do next.

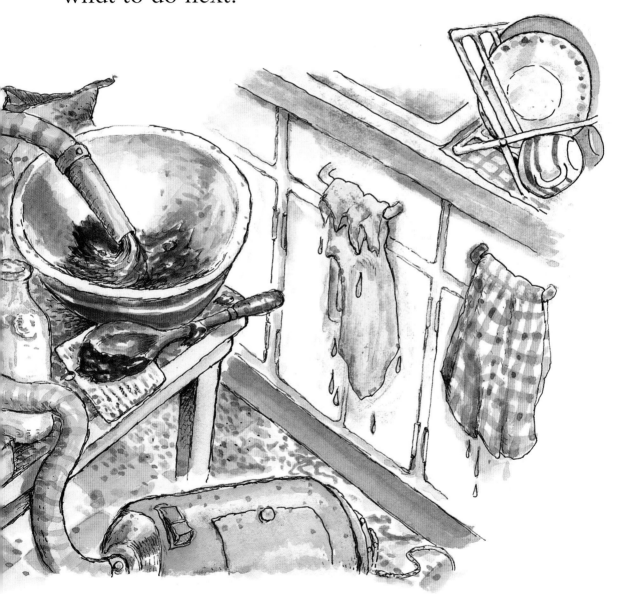

Paddington wasn't the sort of bear to be beaten, and looking at the end of the hose-pipe gave him an idea.

What had happened once could happen again.

He put the hose back on to the wrong end of the cleaner and then he stood back, waiting to see if the cake mix would get blown out.

For a second or two nothing came out, and he was about to poke a spoon down inside to see if that would help, when there was a loud rushing noise.

One moment the kitchen was as clean and shiny as a new pin…

…the next moment it looked as if it had been raining chocolate.

Paddington gazed unhappily around the room. It was in a worse state than before. In fact, he couldn't remember ever having seen such a mess.

He gave a deep
sigh and for the
third time
that day set
to work.

He washed
the breakfast
things. Then he
washed the dusters
and the towels, and
hung them up to dry. Then he scrubbed
the floor and washed the walls and polished
the table and chairs until it all looked as
good as new.

In fact, he cleaned everything except himself.
But by then it was too late, for there was a ring
at the front doorbell.

"Paddington!" cried Mrs Brown. "Whatever
have you been up to? Are you all right? You're
covered in spots."

"*Brown* ones," said Mrs Bird.

Paddington looked
at himself in the hall
mirror and saw for
the first time what a
mess he was in.

"I think I must
have a bad attack
of 'Spring Cleaning
Fever', Mrs Bird,"
he said.

Mrs Bird hurried into the kitchen, but she had to admit she had never seen it looking quite so clean. And if she wondered why Paddington had spots on his duffle coat as well as on his whiskers she didn't say anything.

"I think," she said, "you had better go upstairs and have a nice, hot bath."

Paddington thought that was a very good idea. He felt tired after all his hard work.

Afterwards, when he was safely tucked up in bed, Mrs Brown brought him his supper on a tray.

"You're looking better already," she said. "The rest must be doing you good."

"It isn't so much 'Spring Cleaning' that brings you out in spots, Mrs Brown," said Paddington. "It's all the clearing up you have to do afterwards."

Look out for more fantastic books about Paddington!

HarperCollins *Children's Books*